The Case of the
Detective in Disguise

Read all the Jigsaw Jones Mysteries

Coming Soon

The Case of the
Detective in Disguise

by James Preller
illustrated by Jamie Smith
cover illustration by R. W. Alley

A
LITTLE APPLE
PAPERBACK

SCHOLASTIC INC.
New York Toronto London Auckland Sydney
Mexico City New Delhi Hong Kong

For Dawn Adelman, Maria Barbo, and Bonnie Cutler. With thanks and appreciation for your hard work, skill, and commitment. I couldn't possibly do it without you.

Book design by Dawn Adelman

If you purchased this book without a cover, you should be aware that this book is stolen property. It was reported as "unsold and destroyed" to the publisher, and neither the author nor the publisher has received any payment for this "stripped book."

No part of this work may be reproduced, stored in a retrieval system, or transmitted in any form or by any means, electronic, mechanical, photocopying, recording, or otherwise, without written permission of the publisher. For information regarding permission, write to Scholastic Inc., Attention: Permissions Department, 555 Broadway, New York, NY 10012.

ISBN 0-439-18476-2

Text copyright © 2001 by James Preller. Illustrations © 2001 by Scholastic Inc. All rights reserved. Published by Scholastic Inc. SCHOLASTIC, LITTLE APPLE PAPERBACKS, and associated logos are trademarks and/or registered trademarks of Scholastic Inc.

24 23 22 21 20 19 18 17   08 09 10 11/0

Printed in the U.S.A.   40
First Scholastic printing, January 2001

CONTENTS

Chapter One

A Detective Without a Mystery

It was January. And it hadn't snowed all winter.

If you ask me, that's just *wrong*. Because a winter without snow is like a detective without a mystery. Come to think of it, I was like a detective without a mystery. My piggy bank was starving. I had no money to feed it.

My partner, Mila, and I sat in my basement office. I was on my third glass of grape juice when Mila rose to her feet. "We

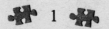

can't sit around all day," she snapped. "We've got to do something."

Mila walked over to our secret hiding place behind the washing machine. She came back carrying a cardboard box. It was labeled:

KEEP OUT AND THAT MEANS YOU!

Mila spilled our box of detective supplies onto the floor. Together, we'd collected some pretty cool stuff. We had walkie-talkies and decoder rings. We had fingerprint kits and how-to books. And we had wigs, clothes, and makeup for disguises.

"Hey, I remember this!" Mila exclaimed. She put a curly green wig on her head. I laughed.

For the next half hour, Mila and I tried on different disguises. Some of them weren't too bad. With a top hat and a hoola hoop, I

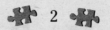

disguised myself as a lion tamer. I even used Rags as a lion and pretended the hoola hoop was a ring of fire. Only Rags wasn't very good at it. He kept licking the hoola hoop instead of jumping through it. Yeesh.

Mila put on a baseball uniform and a catcher's glove. She tucked her hair under a cap. "I'm Mike Piazza!" She laughed.

My mom came down the stairs, carrying a laundry basket. "Oh, how cute! You're playing dress-up!"

"MOM!" I protested. "This isn't dress-up. It's detective work. We're in disguise."

My mom ran her hand through my hair. "I wanted to remind you that I'm volunteering at the children's hospital this week. I arranged for you to stay at Mike and Mary's after school."

"Yeah, sure, fine," I mumbled. Mike and Mary were old family friends who ran a little sandwich shop near school. It was

called Our Daily Bread and Pita. Clever, huh? I liked going there. But at the same time, I wished I didn't have to be baby-sat. It was embarrassing.

I suddenly had a terrific idea. "A lot of people go into that shop," I told Mila. "If we put up a poster, we'll get some business."

"Great idea, Jigsaw!" Mila exclaimed.

We grabbed some poster board, cracked open a new set of markers, and got to

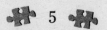

work. Mila was in charge of the fancy lettering. I drew the picture.

"What do you think?" I asked Mila.

She whistled softly. "You're definitely an artist, Jigsaw. But tell me. Is my nose really that big?"

Chapter Two
My Fifth-Grade Buddy

On Monday morning, at 9:14, I was rubbing sleep from my eyes. Mila and I were about to step inside the school when I heard my name.

"Hey, Jigsaw. Think fast!" A football flew toward me. I pretended it was a cold and caught it.

Ben Ewing walked over, smiling happily. "How do you like my new pigskin? It's autographed by Peyton Manning."

"Awesome," Mila said. "He's one of the top quarterbacks in the NFL!"

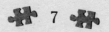 7

Ben grinned proudly. He stretched a hand out to Mila. "You're Mila, right? Jigsaw told me about your detective business. My name's Ben."

Mila blushed shyly. "Can I see your football?"

"Sure," Ben replied. "My father bought it on the Internet. It was a present for my eleventh birthday. I brought it in to show my teacher, Mr. Alonzo."

Ben Ewing was my fifth-grade buddy. In our school, all the younger kids were teamed up with "buddies" from the fifth grade. We worked with our buddies on special projects. I was lucky to have Ben as my buddy. It was like having an extra big brother . . . without the painful wedgies.

"Catch any crooks lately?" Ben asked.

I pulled the poster from my backpack and showed it to Ben. "Business stinks," I admitted. "But I think this will help."

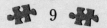 9

NEED A MYSTERY SOLVED?
Call Jigsaw Jones
or Mila Yeh!
For a dollar a day,
we make problems go away.

CALL 555-4523
or 555-4374

Ben was reading the poster when Bobby Solofsky walked up. Bobby lived next door to Ben.

"Hi, Ben!" Bobby said.

"Oh, hi, Bobby," Ben murmured without looking away from the poster.

"I saw you playing catch yesterday!" Bobby said.

"Not now," Ben said. "I'm reading."

Bobby glanced at the poster. He made a sucking sound with his teeth. "Big whoop-de-do," Bobby sneered. "Anybody can be a detective. Besides, his name isn't Jigsaw. It's *Theodore*."

Ben looked annoyed at Bobby. "I don't see *you* solving any mysteries."

Bobby didn't have much to say after that. He just stood quietly, looking down at his shoelaces.

Ben handed back the poster. "Very cool. But I've gotta run. Catch you on the rebound." Ben tucked the football under his arm and took off like a running back.

"Bye, Ben! See you around, pal!" Bobby shouted.

But Ben was long gone.

Chapter Three
Mike and Mary's

I walked home after school instead of taking the bus. That's because I wasn't going home at all. I was headed to Our Daily Bread and Pita. It was just two blocks away.

I was about as happy as a cat in a car wash. Here's the thing. No one had to baby-sit for my brother Billy. He worked at a gas station after school. Daniel and Nick were staying at Barney Fodstock's all week. Hillary got to stay home because she was a "responsible teenager."

As if!

Me? I was the youngest. "The baby." So I had to be baby-sat. I mean, I liked Mike and Mary's. But I was tired of being bossed around.

Mike waved from inside the store. "How ya doing, sport?" he greeted me. He held up an open palm. "Slap me high!"

I jumped up and gave him a high five.

He lowered his hand to waist level. "Slap me low."

I moved to give him a low five, but he pulled his hand away. "Too sloooow!" Mike gushed, laughing.

"Again," I demanded.

This time, I was ready for him. *Slap!*

"Yow! That stung," Mike exclaimed, shaking his hand. "You're getting pretty tough in your old age."

I smiled. It was hard to stay miserable with Mike around. But I'd try.

Mary gave me a hug. "It's good to see you, Jigsaw. It'll be fun to have you around this week."

A detective is like a scientist. He must train himself to be *observant*. I noted the little things, the small details. I looked around the shop with the careful eye of a detective.

There was a long glass counter on the left. Behind that, there was food, the cash register, the yogurt machine, and a big refrigerator filled with cold drinks. On the right, there were a few tables with plastic chairs. That was about it.

Some customers straggled in. "You keep Jigsaw company," Mike told Mary. "I'll take care of this." Mike hustled behind the counter and took their orders. He chatted with the customers and made them laugh. Everybody liked Mike. He claimed it was because he's short and bald. Go figure.

Mary sat down with me. She had long blond hair and eyes as green as AstroTurf. "What's the matter?" she asked. "You seem quiet."

"I like coming here," I answered. "But . . . well . . . I'm tired of being treated like a baby. Everybody else in my family gets to do what they want."

Mary chewed on her lower lip. "Don't let it bother you, Jigsaw. We'll have fun. You'll see."

I slipped the poster out of my backpack. "Can I tape this to your wall? It's for our detective business."

"Sure," Mary answered, eyeing the poster. "You know, maybe it's a good thing you're here. We've had problems lately. I've been thinking about calling the police."

Chapter Four
The Missing Brownies

"The police?!" I exclaimed.

A few customers turned their heads. I recognized some of them from school. There was Bigs Maloney and Lucy Hiller, Shirley Hitchcock, Bobby-Sue Black, and Jake "The Snake" O'Brien. It seemed like everybody came to Mike and Mary's for after-school snacks. Mary's double-chunk chocolate chip cookies were famous.

"Shhh," Mary whispered. "We'll talk later. I've got work to do."

I killed time by walking around the block.

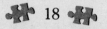

I saw a few kids hanging around by the Dumpster. They were teenagers. It looked like hanging around and doing nothing was their specialty. I made a note of it in my detective journal. I already knew how to spell teenager:

T-R-O-U-B-L-E.

When I returned to the store, all the customers had gone. The after-school rush was over. Mary gestured toward the poster on the wall. She told Mike, "I'm going to hire Jigsaw."

Mike grumbled. But before he could complain, Mary slapped a five-dollar bill on the table.

"Abraham Lincoln," I murmured. "My favorite president."

"It's all yours . . ." Mary said, "if you can catch the brownie bandit."

I wrote in my detective journal:

 19

CLIENTS: MIKE AND MARY.

Below that I wrote,

STOLEN BROWNIES.

"Give me the facts," I told Mary.

She pointed to a large plate on the counter. It was filled with desserts. "It's been going on for about a week now. Every afternoon, we're a few brownies short."

"Are you sure?" I asked.

Mary nodded. "Definitely. This place gets crowded when school lets out. When it slows down, I always notice that there's a couple of brownies missing."

Mary continued, "Lately, we've even run out of brownies. It's bad business. I'm afraid we might lose customers to the store down the block, Barney Black's Sweet Shop. If kids can't get their brownies here, they might shop somewhere else."

I nodded. Mike seemed worried. If kids started going to Barney's, then Mike and Mary would be out of business.

All this talk was making me hungry. "I think I'll need to take a closer look at one of those brownies. It may be a clue."

I bit into a brownie. "We're dealing with a smart thief," I concluded. "These brownies are terrific. Moist, yet chewy."

I soon realized that I'd gobbled up the

whole brownie. "I'll need more evidence," I told Mary. "Can I have another brownie? And may I please have some grape juice, too?"

"Do you think the juice is a clue?" Mike asked.

"Nope. Just thirsty."

Mary laughed. She gave me another brownie and a large grape juice.

"Aren't you guys eating?" I asked.

Mike glanced sadly at Mary. She shook her head. "We're both on strict diets. No more sweets for us."

Mike rubbed his round belly. "We're trying to lose weight."

"Do you have any suspects?" I asked.

"Not really," Mike replied. "We get a lot of people in here. The thief could be anybody."

Mike glanced at his watch. He walked to the door and flipped down a sign: CLOSED.

"We'd better clean up and get you home," he declared.

I thought about the case while helping Mike mop the floor. This was going to be a tough one. A lot of the kids who came here knew me. Plus, my poster — with my picture — was hanging on the wall. No thief was going to try any funny stuff with a top detective hanging around. I decided to go

NEED A MYSTERY SOLVED?
Call Jigsaw Jones
or Mila Yeh!
For a dollar a day
we make problems go away
Call 556-4533
or 556-4574

undercover. And I didn't mean climbing into bed.

I stopped to scribble in my journal:

THE CASE OF THE DETECTIVE IN DISGUISE.

But what disguise should I wear?

Chapter Five
Zigzag Message

Ms. Gleason kept us hopping on Tuesday. No, she didn't give us pogo sticks. But I learned so much that my head grew two hat sizes. First, we did an experiment for our weather unit. We used the scientific method. We had to make *observations* — just like a detective. I knew more about rain, sleet, and snow than our mail carrier, Doris.

Today we studied thunder and lightning.

At circle time, Ms. Gleason read to us about Martin Luther King, Jr. He was a true American hero. He believed in equality for

everybody, no matter what. Ms. Gleason said that the whole school would be decorating the halls this week.

"Why?" asked Ralphie Jordan.

"Think about it, Ralphie," Ms. Gleason said. "What might we be hanging in the halls this week?"

Ralphie's face broke into a loopy smile. "Our underwear?!"

"Oh, Ralphie," groaned Ms. Gleason.

Everybody laughed at Ralphie's joke. After all, *underwear* was just one of those funny words. All the kids in class laughed whenever we heard it. *Stinky* — that was another funny word. Put them together, *stinky underwear,* and suddenly you've got a classroom full of kids rolling on the floor, laughing their heads off.

Ms. Gleason asked us, "Whose birthday are we celebrating next week?"

"I know!" Danika Starling exclaimed. "Martin Luther King, Jr.'s!"

"That's right, Danika," Ms. Gleason said. "Our principal, Mr. Rogers, gave room 201 a special assignment. We'll be decorating the banner for the lobby."

Ms. Gleason pulled out a long roll of paper. It read:

JOIN HANDS FOR KINDNESS AND JUSTICE!

I raised my hand. "Can I color it?"

"Me, too!" Bigs Maloney said.

"No, me!" Lucy Hiller shouted.

"Slow down, everybody," Ms. Gleason said, laughing. "All of you will get a chance to color in a letter. Ralphie, Kim, Mike, Athena — bring the banner and crayons into the hall. When you finish a letter, pick someone to replace you. Everybody else, take out your writing folders."

Before I started on my story, I jotted a quick note to Mila. It was in code:

C N O S L E Y Y T R C D
A Y U O V M M S E Y O E

It was called a zigzag code. The words were written up and down on two lines. I wrote the first letter, C. Beneath it, I wrote the second letter, A. Then I started on the first line again. To make it a little tougher, I didn't put any spaces between the words.

I handed the note to Mila. A moment later, she smiled and slid a finger across her nose. That was our secret signal. She understood the message.

Soon our fifth-grade buddies were coming through the door. Ms. Gleason sent half of our class down the hall to meet with their buddies in Mr. Alonzo's fifth-grade classroom. That's how everybody fit.

I watched as the fifth-graders came in. There was Jimmy the Weasel, Rajib Manna, Henry Sosa, and Scooby Wendell. There was Bobbie-Sue Black, Babs Barbo, Silu Chang, and Kelsey Saperstein, giggling as usual. And, of course, my buddy Ben Ewing.

The minute I saw Ben, I knew something was wrong.

I will
stand up
for
people

Chapter Six

A Stone in My Shoe

We got started on our projects right away. First, we traced our hand on a piece of construction paper. Then our fifth-grade buddies cut it out very carefully. Fifth-graders are good at that stuff.

Ms. Gleason explained, "Our entire school is celebrating Martin Luther King, Jr.'s birthday. We're calling it the Peace and Kindness Challenge. We're asking every student to think about what you could do to make a more peaceful world."

"Could it be *anything* we want?" Geetha asked.

"Yes," Ms. Gleason answered. "Like Martin Luther King, I want you all to dream of a better world. Think about what YOU can do to help. Talk it over with your buddies. Then write your answer on the helping hands. Every class in school is doing it. We'll hang our hands up and down the halls."

After a lot of discussion, we had a great collection of ideas. Everyone except me. I wasn't so sure that I could make a better world all by myself. After all, I was a detective, not Hercules. Here's what everybody else wrote:

I will make the world a better place by helping
the homeless.
— Lucy

I will be a doctor and help sick people.
— Geetha

I will talk to kids who don't have anyone to talk to.
— Jasper

Plant flowers everywhere!
— Joey

If someone punches me I won't punch back.
— Helen

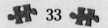 33

I will stand up for people.
— Bigs

I could create world peace by
making friends.
— Danika

By putting a smile on my face!
— Athena

We should protect animals around the world.
— Nicole

I will not push in the cubbies.
— Bobby

Talk to kids who are lonely.
— Ralphie

I am going to pick up litter.
— Kim

I WILL BE NICE ON THE PLAYGROUND.
— MIKE

I don't think people should be made fun of.
— Eddie

I will give food to poor people.
— Mila

Unfortunately, my buddy Ben wasn't much help. He was too miserable. I tried to cheer him up. I made goofy faces. I cracked jokes. I even fell off my chair on purpose. But nothing worked.

"What's wrong?" I finally asked.

"Someone stole my football," Ben said.

"Mila and I will help you get it back," I offered.

Suddenly Bobby Solofsky nudged me out of the way. "I'm a better detective

35

than him," Bobby bragged. "I'll find your football."

Oh, brother. Mr. Wonderful — Bobby Solofsky. He'd been a stone in my shoe since kindergarten. Solofsky always tried to trick me. And he always failed. I wondered what he was up to this time.

"Forget it, guys," Ben said, shaking his head sadly. "My ball is gone forever."

"Don't give up," I urged. "I'll help you get justice!"

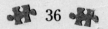

"Don't listen to him." Bobby snorted. "I *guarantee* I'll find that football for you."

"Who invited you, Solofsky?" I snarled.

"Guys! Guys!" Ben interrupted. "I don't care who solves the case. Just get my football back. Please."

"May the best detective win," Bobby said. He smiled wickedly. "And that means me!"

Chapter Seven
Red Cap

Instead of going straight into Our Daily Bread that afternoon, I decided to swing around the back and have another look around. There was a small parking lot behind the store, with enough room for about twenty cars. There was a big brown Dumpster. Beyond the lot were the back-yards of a few houses. As I guessed, I saw the same kids as yesterday. It didn't look like a meeting of Boy Scout Troop #67, if you know what I mean. Yeesh, teenagers.

I gave Mike and Mary's back door a pull.

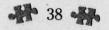

Nothing doing. I yanked harder. The heavy, metal door didn't budge. Good, I thought to myself. The thief isn't sneaking in the back door.

"They keep it locked," a voice said.

I glanced over my shoulder. A boy with a red cap stood nearby. "What are you doing, short stuff?" he asked.

I looked him up and down. There was a lot of "up" to look at. This kid was tall, all right. I decided to get out of there, fast. The next thing I remember, Red Cap grabbed me by the shoulder. "Hey, I asked a question," he snarled. "Why are you poking around back here?"

Red Cap gave my shoulder a *squeeze*. I felt like an orange. "If you're trying to get juice out of me," I said, "it's not going to work."

The boy's dark eyes pierced through me. He grinned, then let go of my shoulder.

"Get lost," he said. "Scram."

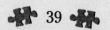

39

So, well, I scrammed. It wasn't like I enjoyed his company.

When I got back, the store was jammed with customers. I strolled in, nodded at Mike, and kept right on walking. I didn't want anyone to notice me. I stepped into the back room.

When I came back out five minutes later, even my pet parakeet wouldn't have recognized me. Of course, I didn't have a pet parakeet. But never mind that. I wore a long, tan raincoat. I turned up the collar, pulled a hat over my eyes, and shoved my hands deep into the pockets.

A fake beard covered my face.

Sure, I may have looked strange. But no one could tell that I was a detective in disguise. I sat with my back to the counter and slipped on the rearview sunglasses. They were like regular glasses, except small mirrors were taped to the lenses. This way, I could face forward but still see what was going on behind me! I opened a comic book and pretended to read. I had a perfect view of the dessert tray.

For the next hour, I tried to observe everything. A steady stream of customers flowed into the store. I never took my eyes off the brownies. It was the perfect setup. Except for one thing. The fake beard made me hotter than a woolly mammoth in a pizza oven.

Mike had been right. The store did get all

kinds of people. But the only ones touching the brownies were Mike and Mary.

I made notes in my journal. I saw that Bobby-Sue Black was here again. She bought a brownie.

It made me wonder.

Suddenly, I stiffened. A familiar voice said: "I saw a kid snooping around out back," the voice told Mike. "I figured you should know about it."

It was Red Cap.

Chapter Eight

Undercover

That night I talked to Mila on the phone. I told her about Ben's stolen football. "The problem is, I'm stuck at the sandwich shop all week. You've got to look for clues without me.

"Try to find witnesses," I advised. "Bobby lives across the street from Ben. Mike Radcliffe lives near Ben, too. Talk to Mike. Poke around. Something will turn up."

"You can count on me," Mila replied. Then she asked, "How's your case coming?"

"Don't ask," I said.

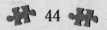

"I just did," she stated.

Oh, brother. "I wouldn't call it a good day," I said. "Two more brownies were stolen — but I didn't see it happen. The store gets so crowded, it's hard to see everything. Some teenager with a red cap nearly squeezed me to a pulp. And I've got a rash on my face from wearing that lousy beard."

"I'd call that a bad day," Mila said.

"Let me ask you something," I said. "Bobby-Sue Black — what do you know about her?"

"Very little," Mila said. "She's in Mr. Alonzo's class. Why?"

"Do you know Barney Black's Sweet Shop?" I asked.

"Sure," Mila said. "It has great candy. But you should ask Bobby-Sue about that. Barney Black is her father."

"Her father!" I exclaimed. "Then why was she buying a brownie at Mike and Mary's?"

"Don't ask me," Mila said. "Ask Bobby-Sue."

I made a few more notes in my journal. I wrote the name Bobby-Sue Black and circled it. Could she be the one stealing the brownies? I couldn't be sure. But I knew Mila was right. I'd have to have a little talk with Bobby-Sue.

I came up with a better disguise the next day. I put on an apron and carried around a broom. It looked like I had a job cleaning

up. But I was really a bodyguard for a plate of brownies.

I had to admit it. I was beginning to like hanging around the store. It didn't feel like being baby-sat at all. Mike and Mary were fun. They had goofy nicknames for all the customers.

For example, there was Warm Cookie Guy. He came in at 3:30 every day and ordered the exact same thing. He liked his cookie warmed up in the microwave. It drove Mary nuts. Mike's favorite was the Sourpuss. She was a thin, sad-eyed lady who was always angry about something — the weather (too cold), the work (too busy), even the brownies (too fattening).

"What about the tall kid with the red cap?" I asked.

Mike smiled. "Oh, that's Marc. Real good kid. He lives in one of the houses behind the parking lot."

"I better have a talk with him," I remarked. "I don't trust teenagers."

Mike laughed. "That's funny, because Marc doesn't trust you, either. He came in here yesterday and told me he saw a suspicious kid out back. Just being a good neighbor, I guess."

"I guess," I answered.

I began to get into the routine of the store. Certain things happened every day. Mike *always* threw out the empty boxes in the afternoon. Then we always sat down together for a snack before cleanup. Mike called it our time "to shoot the breeze." Mike was a great talker. He could carry on a two-way conversation all by himself. It was a good thing. Because half the time Mary wasn't even listening.

Mike took a small bite of his granola bar, then tossed it into the garbage can. "Tastes like tree bark," he complained. "I'm starving, Mary! I hate this diet! I don't want

to be skinny and miserable. I'd rather be plump and jolly."

Just then, Bobby Solofsky came into the store with Mike Radcliff. "Hey, Theodore," he crowed. "Any luck finding Ben's football?"

I didn't bother to reply.

Solofsky laughed, like he already knew the answer. "I didn't think so, *Theodore*!" I hated when he called me that. They bought vanilla milk shakes, then left the store.

It was how I liked Solofsky best: *Leaving*.

Chapter nine

Counting Alligators

I forgot my lunch on Thursday. That meant I had to eat the hot lunch — a cheeseburger that looked like it was left over from the Jurassic period.

"I'd rather eat an old shoe," I groaned.

Helen Zuckerman plopped down beside me. It could only mean one thing. Helen had a new joke to tell. "Hey, Jigsaw," Helen said. "How do they stop crime at McDonald's?"

I shrugged.

"With a burger alarm!" Helen shouted. "Get it? *Burger alarm!*"

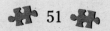

I got it and told her so.

Mila sat down opposite us. I was relieved. "How's our case coming?" I asked her.

Mila told me all about it. Ben Ewing said he left his football outside by accident. In the morning, the football was gone.

"Any clues?"

"Not much," Mila said. I could hear the frustration in her voice. "There's one thing bothering me, though. Every time I see

Mike Radcliff, he's too busy too talk. I'm beginning to think he's avoiding me."

I told Mila about the brownie bandit. "I don't know who's doing it," I admitted. "The only people I've seen touching the brownies are Mike and Mary."

"Hmmm," Mila said.

I wanted to ask her what "hmmm" meant. Was it a good "hmmm" or a bad "hmmm"? But I wanted to escape from Helen's jokes even more. One bad joke a day was enough for me.

I caught up with Bobby-Sue Black by the bike racks after school. I told her that I'd seen her in Mike and Mary's store.

"And? So?" Bobby-Sue said with a yawn.

"So I'm wondering why you bought a brownie at Mike and Mary's. That is, IF you bought it."

Bobby-Sue scowled. "Whaddya mean . . . *if* I bought it?"

Bobby-Sue knew exactly what I meant. "I

don't steal, if that's what you are trying to say," she said firmly.

Finally, she sighed. "Look, if you tell my father, I'm dead. But Mary's brownies are delicious. I'd rather pay for hers than eat my dad's for free."

"Moist and chewy," I said.

"Yup," Bobby-Sue agreed. "My dad's brownies are as dry as sawdust." She paused. "You won't tell anyone I said that, will you?"

"My lips are sealed," I answered. And that was that. She might be the thief, she might not. But by the look in her eyes, I'd say she was an honest person.

That afternoon I disguised myself as a football player. I watched Mike and Mary's customers come and go. There were twenty brownies sold. But by the end of the day, there was an extra one missing. Something was wrong. A piece of the puzzle was missing. Then it hit me. I remembered my words to Mila: "The only people touching the brownies are Mike and Mary."

It was true. Except for today. Mary's customers didn't buy any brownies. She never touched them. Just then, Mike left to throw out the garbage. I watched the clock carefully. He returned after four minutes and twenty-six seconds. I jotted it down in my journal:

4 minutes, 26 seconds
Check it out

I decided to retrace his steps. I walked down the basement steps. Out the back door. Over to the Dumpster. Then back again. I counted to myself the whole time: "One alligator, two alligator, three alligator . . ."

I was back inside after seventy-four alligators. I did the math in my journal. One minute was sixty alligators.

74 - 60 = 14

It took me only one minute and fourteen seconds. Why did the same trip take Mike almost four and a half minutes?

It was time to make peace with Red Cap,

er, I mean, Marc. I didn't see him at first, until I looked up. He was leaning out of his second-floor window, just watching the world go by. It gave me an idea.

I called him down and we had a little chat. It turned out that Mike was right. Marc was a good guy, once you got to know him. I told him I was a detective working on a case. We talked about the stolen brownies. I offered him a dollar if he'd help me.

Marc said he'd do it for free.

"See you tomorrow," I said.

Marc winked. "Sure thing . . . Detective Jones."

Chapter Ten

Strange Weather

The next morning, Mila and I saw Bobby Solofsky on the bus. He sat in the back with Mike Radcliff. They seemed as happy as dentists at a candy store.

When the bus dropped us off, Bobby and Mike raced in our direction. "Hey, guys. Wait up."

"What now, Solofsky?" I groaned.

Bobby waved at Ben Ewing across the school yard. "Show him!" Bobby shouted.

Ben smiled brightly. He reached into his

backpack and pulled out his prized football. "Catch!" he said to me.

I dropped the ball.

"Poor Theodore," Bobby said. "It looks like you fumbled the case this time."

Bobby pulled out a crisp, clean, five-dollar bill. "Ben gave it to me," Bobby said. "Because I'm such a great detective."

Then he laughed.

Long and loud.

It was like talking to Helen Zuckerman.

I didn't see what was so funny.

"Not so fast, Solofsky," Mila said. "Something fishy is going on around here. How did you solve the case?"

"Easy," Bobby bragged. "Mike was a witness. He saw the kids do it."

Mike chimed in. "I saw the whole thing from my bedroom window."

Mila was right. This case was fishy. In fact, it smelled like Sea World. Sure, Mike Radcliff was a decent guy. But he'd do anything Bobby told him. I didn't trust him.

Mike explained that he saw three big kids walk on Ben's lawn. They took the ball, then hid it in the bushes. Mike said he went out and got the ball before the kids had time to come back for it.

"Maybe that's what happened," I said. "But why did you wait so long before giving the ball back?"

Bobby put his arm around Mike's

shoulders. "Mike was scared," Bobby said. "Those teenagers were awful big."

I didn't argue. "What time was it when you saw them?"

Mike glanced at Bobby. "About, um, eight-thirty."

"You must be part owl," I said. "Because it's hard to see in the dark."

"It was a full moon," Bobby quickly replied.

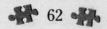

"Not quite, Solofsky," Mila replied. "The clouds were too thick on Monday night. You remember all that rain we had. Besides, I checked the neighborhood. The nearest streetlight was broken."

Even Ben seemed a little curious now. "Why did they *hide* the football, anyway? Why didn't they just take it? I don't get it."

Bobby waved a hand, like swatting away a pesky fly. "When the thieves picked up the football, a set of car headlights turned up the street. They must have decided to ditch the stolen ball until later."

"Your story is like Swiss cheese," I said. "It's full of holes. What I want to know is: *How did Mike see in the dark?*"

All eyes turned to Mike Radcliff. He swallowed hard and stammered, "I was, um, reading at my desk. And, um, I guess I fell asleep. Then suddenly, I awoke to a

crash of thunder. And I looked out the window. Lightning lit the sky. That's when I saw the teenagers take the ball."

"That's pretty strange weather," I said. "The thunder woke you up. Then the lightning came. And then you saw the robbers?"

"What's the matter, Theodore?" Bobby sniped. "Do you need me to explain it in slow motion? Yes, he heard thunder. Yes, he looked out the window. Yes, there was lightning. Yes, he saw the robbers. Case closed. Mystery solved."

Mila angrily jabbed a finger at Solofsky. "You guys are lying — and I can prove it!"

Chapter Eleven
With a Little Help
from My Friends

Bobby shook his head. "Let's go, Mike. We're not sticking around for this."

"Oh, yes you are," Ben threatened.

Bobby and Mike didn't dare move.

"Go on, Mila," Ben said politely.

Mila folded her arms across her chest. "We've been studying weather in Ms. Gleason's class," she told Ben.

"We learned about light and sound. Light travels faster than sound. Mike's story doesn't hold up. He said he awoke to thunder. Then he saw lightning. Weather

 66

doesn't work that way. Lightning always comes first. That's why I know he's lying."

Solofsky stood tight-lipped. He wasn't going to say a word. But Mike Radcliff looked at Ben towering over him and turned pale. "It was all Bobby's idea!" Mike confessed. "He wanted to fake a crime. Then he'd solve it and be the hero!"

In a gush of words, Mike explained everything. He saw the football on the lawn with Bobby. They decided to "borrow" it. "Bobby was jealous," Mike explained to Ben. "He didn't like that you were becoming friends with Jigsaw."

Ben shook his head sadly. Then he held out his hand. "Cough it up, Bobby," he demanded.

Solofsky pulled out a five-dollar bill. Ben plucked it from his fingertips and handed it to Mila. "Thanks," Ben told her. "You deserve it."

One mystery solved.

One more to go.

I ran to the store right after school. I met Marc in the parking lot and lent him a walkie-talkie. The plan was set. Marc went up to his back window and waited for my signal.

As usual, Mike went outside to throw out the garbage at around five o'clock. The moment he left, I reached for my walkie-talkie.

"He's on his way," I whispered.

"I hear you loud and clear," Marc replied. "Over and out."

Mike returned about five minutes later.

A few minutes after that, Marc strolled in the front door. He looked at me and winked.

I nodded back.

Marc and I walked up to Mike and Mary. "We just solved the case," I announced.

Mary's eyebrow lifted.

Mike's jaw dropped.

"It took me a while," I admitted, looking directly at Mike. "It never occurred to me that you'd be stealing from yourself."

It's always the little things that give a thief away. I picked a brownie crumb off Mike's collar. "Some diet," I said. "Every day you sneak a brownie or two into an empty box. When you go outside to throw out the garbage, you have a little snack."

"But . . ." Mike stammered.

"Marc saw everything," I said. "Don't bother denying it."

Mary didn't seem too mad. To tell the truth, she didn't even seem all that surprised. She just shook her head and laughed.

Mike tried to defend himself. "Mary, darling, poopsie doll. You can't blame me. Everybody knows that you make the best brownies in the world. I couldn't help myself!"

Mary slipped a brownie off the plate and popped a piece into her mouth. "Oh, well," she said, giving Mike a big hug. "I guess I like my men plump and jolly. No more diets for you!"

My mom came and picked me up a little later. She loved hearing about the brownie bandit. I hadn't seen her laugh so hard in a long while. "We'd better get going," she said. "It's starting to snow."

"Snow?!"

I raced to the window. A few white flakes fluttered from the clouds. The case was over. In one day, we'd solved two mysteries. And I'd made a new friend — a teenager, no less. And like Martin Luther King, Jr., I suddenly knew how to make the world a better place.

The same way I do puzzles.

The same way I solve mysteries.

Just one piece at a time.

Here's a sneak peek at the next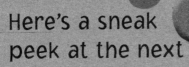

The Case of the Bicycle Bandit

by James Preller

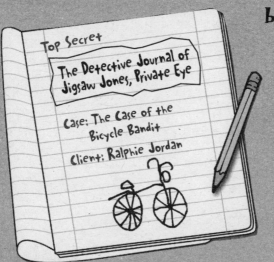

Top Secret

The Detective Journal of
Jigsaw Jones, Private Eye

Case: The Case of the
Bicycle Bandit

Client: Ralphie Jordan

Someone stole Ralphie Jordan's rusty old bicycle. Jigsaw and Mila hit the trail to track down the thief. But one piece of the puzzle doesn't fit. Who would take a hand-me-down bike? Solving this case is an uphill ride for ace detectives Jigsaw and Mila.

Coming Soon

3 1901 04563 9012